It was the end of summer. The katydids were still buzzing when I finally summoned up the courage to ask my dad if I could stay with him and Gramma for the school year instead of going back to California to be with Mom like always. "Your mother would miss you, Trisha, but I will talk to her," Dad said.

I had a reason for staying. A good reason.

To the wonder of Mrs. Peterson and my tribe.

Patricia Lee Gauch, Editor

PHILOMEL BOOKS
A division of Penguin Young Readers Group.
Published by The Penguin Group.
Penguin Group (USA) Inc., 375 Hudson Street, New York, NY 10014, U.S.A.
Penguin Group (Canada), 90 Eglinton Avenue East, Suite 700, Toronto, Ontario M4P 2Y3, Canada (a division of Pearson Penguin Canada Inc.).
Penguin Books Ltd, 80 Strand, London WC2R 0RL, England.
Penguin Ireland, 25 St. Stephen's Green, Dublin 2, Ireland (a division of Penguin Books Ltd).
Penguin Group (Australia), 250 Camberwell Road, Camberwell, Victoria 3124, Australia (a division of Pearson Australia Group Pty Ltd).
Penguin Books India Pvt Ltd, 11 Community Centre, Panchsheel Park, New Delhi - 110 017, India.
Penguin Group (NZ), 67 Apollo Drive, Rosedale, North Shore 0632, New Zealand (a division of Pearson New Zealand Ltd).
Penguin Books (South Africa) (Pty) Ltd, 24 Sturdee Avenue, Rosebank, Johannesburg 2196, South Africa.
Penguin Books Ltd, Registered Offices: 80 Strand, London WC2R 0RL, England.

Published simultaneously in Canada. Manufactured in China by South China Printing Co. Ltd.

Design by Semadar Megged. Text set in 16-point Adobe Jenson.
The illustrations are rendered in pencils and markers.

Library of Congress Cataloging-in-Publication Data
Polacco, Patricia.   The junkyard wonders / Patricia Polacco.
p. cm. Summary: Inspired by a teacher who believes each of them is a genius, a class of special-needs students invents something that could convince the whole school they are justifiably proud to be "Junkyard Wonders." [1. Teachers—Fiction. 2. Schools—Fiction. 3. Inventions—Fiction. 4. Interpersonal relations—Fiction. 5. Self-esteem—Fiction. 6. People with disabilities— Fiction.] I. Title.
PZ7.P75186Jtt 2010   [Fic]—dc22 2009027145
ISBN 978-0-399-25078-1
1 3 5 7 9 10 8 6 4 2

The Junkyard Wonders

Patricia Polacco

PHILOMEL BOOKS *An Imprint of Penguin Group (USA) Inc.*

My heart sang as I walked to school with all of the kids on my gramma's block on the first day of school. My mother and father had decided that I could stay—just for one year—there with my father and Gramma in Michigan. In my old school in California, the kids all knew that I had just learned to read . . . that I used to be dumb. Everyone knew that I was always in special classes. Here no one would know. No one would tease me. And I already had a new friend: Kay.

But when I got to the front steps of the school, all of the neighborhood kids ran off to their classes, and when I saw Kay and waved to her, she didn't wave back. I just stood there not knowing where to go, and when I showed two strange girls my class card, they got funny looks on their faces.

"You're in Mrs. Peterson's class," they said. "Upstairs, Room 206."

Room 206. I found it. In the classroom, a gawky boy I'd never seen before yelled out, "Hey! The name's Thom, not spelled T-o-m but T-h-o-m. Sit here next to me." He had huge dark-rimmed glasses that magnified his eyes. I sat down and looked around. Everyone seemed really different in one way or another. I couldn't put my finger on it.

Suddenly, everyone snapped to attention. Our teacher was standing in the doorway.

Short and stout, she seemed a little scary, brusque. But her eyes . . . her eyes were friendly. I was sure of that.

She walked up to the podium at the front of the room and slammed an enormous dictionary on top of it. Then she adjusted her glasses, and without saying hello or how are you, she started reading in this no-nonsense voice.

"The definition of genius," she began.

"Genius is neither learned nor acquired.
It is knowing without experience.
It is risking without fear of failure.
It is perception without touch.
It is understanding without research.
It is certainty without proof.
It is ability without practice.
It is invention without limitations.
It is imagination without boundaries.
It is creativity without constraints.
It is . . . extraordinary intelligence!"

Then she took a deep breath and slammed the book shut so hard, it sounded like a gunshot.

"Welcome to the junkyard. I am your teacher, Mrs. Peterson." She started walking around the room, looking at each of us. "I want you all to write the definition on the blackboard. Post it on your mirrors. Look at it every day. Memorize it! The definition describes every one of you."

At recess that day, I couldn't wait to ask Thom, "Why is our class called the junkyard?"

"Because we are . . . didn't you notice . . . all of us are . . . different. You know . . . odd. Like stuff in a junkyard." He turned toward the playground. "See that super-tall kid over there? That's Jody Beach. He's got some disease that makes him grow too fast. He's my bodyguard; no one picks on me when he's around." He smiled. "Over there, that kid? That's Gibbie McDonald. He has Tourette's. There's Stuart Bean. He has diabetes. Me? Well, I have trouble seeing. They call me Sissy Boy because, even so, I love ballet! It's my life."

"I take ballet, too, at least I did in California."

"I knew there was something about you I liked," Thom said.

I felt I had found a soul mate in Thom, and since he thought Jody was nifty . . . so did I.

But it only helped a little.

When I got home that night, I told Dad and Gramma about my day. I tried to be brave and not let them know how sad I really was. But just as Dad was tucking me in at bedtime, I finally burst into tears. "Oh, Daddy, I've been put in a special class again. It's called the junkyard."

"Junkyard! What junkyard?" my dad asked.

"That's what everybody calls our class."

"Darlin'," my dad said, "you are not a quitter. Stick it out for a month. If the class doesn't get better, I promise I'll send you back to California."

I didn't tell him that when I tried to sit with Kay and her friends at lunch, she said that junkyard kids couldn't sit at their table.

The next day, Mrs. Peterson arrived in class with a basket full of small glass bottles.

"Today," she said, "we are going to determine your tribes." She gave us each a vial.

"Tip some of the liquid on your wrist. Hmmmm. Smell? Some of you smell like lemons, some cinnamon, some almonds. Now, can you smell someone who has the same scent as you? They will be part of your tribe for the year!"

I sniffed my own wrist: vanilla!

We all strolled around the classroom, sniffing each other's wrists. I sniffed a boy's wrist who was wearing a homespun shirt, and he sniffed mine. "Vanilla!" we both said.

"My name's Gilbert McDonald—call me Gibbie." Then the two of us fanned out. I found a girl who smelled like vanilla.

"Looks like you are in my tribe," I chirped. She just smiled, but didn't answer me.

Gibbie came over with Thom. "Vanilla!" he announced. "My bodyguard Jody is, too."

So Thom, Gibbie, Jody and I were a tribe! I asked the shy girl her name. She wrote it down on a piece of paper: Ravanne Salze.

Thom told me later that she hadn't spoken as long as he had known her.

From then on, whenever there was a project to be done, Mrs. Peterson had the tribes work together.

Ravanne never talked, but she was a whiz at math. Gibbie had tics and shouted for no reason sometimes, but his father was a professor of engineering and Gibbie loved to build things— boy, was he smart. Jody loved reading . . . everything! Particularly poetry. He even wrote poems of his own. Thom made all of us laugh. He was so clever. Me, of course, I could draw. So I became the official journal keeper—the borders were filled with my drawings.

It wasn't long before Thom, Jody, Gibbie, Ravanne and I were best friends. We did almost everything together.

Even after school. We visited Jody, who lived out on a farm east of town. His mother decorated cakes, and she was working on the tallest wedding cake I had ever seen. We all helped her.

One night, Gibbie's dad set up a telescope in his back field and invited the whole class over to look. We could see Saturn with our naked eyes, but with the telescope we could see Saturn's rings!

We never did go to Ravanne's house; she lived in a foster home, and I don't think she was too happy there, but her foster mother let her paint beautiful designs on silk from an old World War II parachute, which she brought to school to show us.

My dad arranged for the whole class to go to a neighbor's farm and have a hayride that took us way off into the fields.

Our class was special, all right. The junkyard kids were pretty amazing to begin with, and Mrs. Peterson showed us how to shine. She even helped us make badges that said "The Junkyard Wonders."

"So you can be proud of who you are!" she said.

That day we got the badges, this mean boy came running up to us. "Weirdos, retards, now you even wear dumbbell pins!" A boy named Barton Poole grabbed the pin off my shirt. I started to cry, but then Thom and Gibbie ran at Barton and his friends.

"Right," one of his friends said. "Now twinkle toes and duh . . . duh . . . duh the jerking fool are going to hurt us. We are so scared!"

Just about then, Jody—big, wonderful Jody—appeared from nowhere. The mean boys sure backed off.

"Someday you aren't gonna have this freak to guard you," Barton snarled as he stalked away.

That day, Mrs. Peterson could see that we were badly shaken.

Gibbie finally spoke up. "Mrs. Peterson," he said, "we're all junkyard kids, even though you try to make us feel better about it. We're throwaways, junk, and everyone knows it."

"Oh, my dear, that's where you are wrong," she said wistfully. "Every one of you is my wonder! . . . Don't you realize what a junkyard really is?"

"A place for things that nobody wants," Jody answered.

"Oh, it is a place full of wondrous possibilities! What some see as bent and broken throwaways are actually amazing things waiting to be made into something new. Something unexpected. Something surprising."

We all looked puzzled.

"All right, class, get your coats. We are walking to the Melvin Beach junkyard right now," she exclaimed.

At the junkyard, Mrs. Peterson stopped us. "Now form into your tribes. Then, collect everything that you think could be made into something new. Remember, Wonders, here's your chance. Forget what the object was . . . imagine what it could be!"

Each of the tribes set off across the junkyard, collecting wheels, doors, handles, latches. We Vanillas hadn't gotten just the right junk, though, until almost the end of our visit. As Jody, Ravanne, Thom and I were climbing over our last pile of assorted junk, Gibbie called to us. He was standing under a shed roof, looking up.

There, hanging from the roof strut, was an old wrecked model airplane.

"Gib, that's just an old torn-up plane," Thom said, turning to leave.

"No," Gibbie said. "It's a beauty. I see it. We are going to rebuild it into something bigger, better . . . something wonderful . . . something that will defy gravity itself. This plane is gonna fly all the way to the moon."

There was such wonder in his eyes that we knew we had just what we needed.

For the next few weeks, during the last hour of our class time, we worked on our new inventions. As we hammered and sawed and cut, Mrs. Peterson read to us: *Great Expectations*, *David Copperfield*, and sometimes poetry.

But every day Mrs. Peterson reminded us, "Some people look at things the way they are and cry, 'Why!' But I want you to look at things and see what they could be and ask, 'Why not?'"

Gibbie was the boss of our plane project. We removed all the outer skin, built in new balsa struts, and repaired a lot of the skeleton. Ravanne replaced the old skin with pure silk. Finally, we painted the rebuilt plane with low-resistance lacquer. But would it fly?

The day came when we were to present our stupendous projects. The Cinnamon Tribe was first. They unveiled a tangled sculpture of hollow tubes.

"Well," Mrs. Peterson asked the Cinnamons, "what is your invention?"

"A Vibraphonium!" the Cinnamons called out.

It took three people to play it. Fabulous!

The Almonds made a Hanging Wall Maze full of levers, fulcrums and counterweights. When ball bearings were loaded into the top, they clattered down, bounced, shivered and jumped as they ran through the maze. Stupendous!

When the Lemons uncovered their device, none of us could figure out what it was. "This IS perpetual movement!" Dallas Schaeffer gave his invention a shove. It leaned way forward, ringing bells, pulling at springs, and twisting back and forth. We must have watched that thing for fifteen minutes. It just did not stop.

When it was the Vanillas' turn, Gibbie pulled the covering off.

"But that's just an old model airplane!" Booth Schiffer called out.

"Wrong," Gibbie shouted back. "This here airplane is gonna defy gravity. This baby is goin' all the way to the moon!"

Everyone laughed. Mrs. Peterson spoke up. "If Gilbert says it is destined for the moon, I, for one, believe him!"

"Come on, Gibbie, will that thing fly?" someone shouted.

"Oh, it will fly, all right—we flew it like a kite off of Putnam's hill," Jody trumpeted.

We had.

"That was off a hill; for it to fly by itself, though, we need a propulsion unit."

"He means a motor," I added. "And we found the perfect one—it will take the plane right into the sky. . . . The trouble is, it's expensive."

That's when the tribes stepped in. All of them. Mrs. Peterson asked the whole class if they'd help raise money for the motor. Everyone cheered! It was unanimous: they would.

For the next few weeks all of the moms made cakes and cookies and sold them at bake sales. Our dads sponsored car washes. All of us junkyard kids used things we had gotten from Mr. Beach's and made gadgets to sell.

By that spring we had made enough money to buy that perfect motor. The next thing to do was set a date for launch. We wanted everyone in school to see it. That's when Gibbie thought of the school science fair.

"Perfect," Jody said. He had started missing a lot of school, not feeling well. When he was there, Ravanne was at his side. Sometimes she even helped him climb the stairs. "We could launch it from the school roof, and it would fly right over the field where the fair is!" The class cheered.

"Maybe," Mrs. Peterson said. "But wait. This magnificent airship has to have a name."

Everyone started calling out names like "Fabulous Flyer" and "Windy Wings."

Jody stood up—he sure looked pale. "I think she needs to be called the Junkyard Wonder . . . because we made it out of junk and because we Junkyard Wonders made it. That plane is us!"

It was just a week later when Mrs. Peterson was late. She was never late! Her eyes were red, and she looked sad.

"Please sit down. I have some very bad news. . . ." There was silence. "We have lost Jody Beach. He passed away last night in his sleep." Then she put her face in her hands and cried.

"How?" I managed to sputter. Ravanne and I held hands.

"Jody had a disease that made his body grow faster than it should. It just kept growing and growing so fast that his dear heart couldn't keep up. It just gave out," Mrs. Peterson answered.

Later that day, the whole class went to the woods behind the school to collect flowers and to remember Jody.

"Now I know what the plane has to be called," a voice called out. At first, we couldn't figure out who was talking. Then, to our shock, we realized it was Ravanne. None of us knew she could talk. "He wanted it to be called the Junkyard Wonder. That's what it has to be." Tears rolled down her cheeks.

All of us agreed.

Gibbie's dad mounted the motor on the machine and placed it on a table at the back of his workshop.

When we saw it, we all gathered around. It was so beautiful. We tried it out, more than once, from the hill in back of Gibbie's house. It seemed to work. But would it work from the roof of the school on fair day? And would we even get a chance to try? The stairway to the roof was always locked. Maybe Mr. Weeks, the janitor, could help us get to the roof.

"I think he will," Mrs. Peterson said. "But it will have to be a secret."

The day before the fair, we could hardly contain ourselves. Would newspapers be there? Scientists from a nearby university? We huddled together out on the playground, chattering about our plans for the launch.

"Cheese it, look who's listening," Thom warned.

It was Barton Poole—he'd heard everything.

He leaned in to Gibbie's face. "Your dad wears skirts!" Then he sneered. "And no one's allowed on the school roof. Got it? No one! And I'm telling the principal about your stupid plans. . . ."

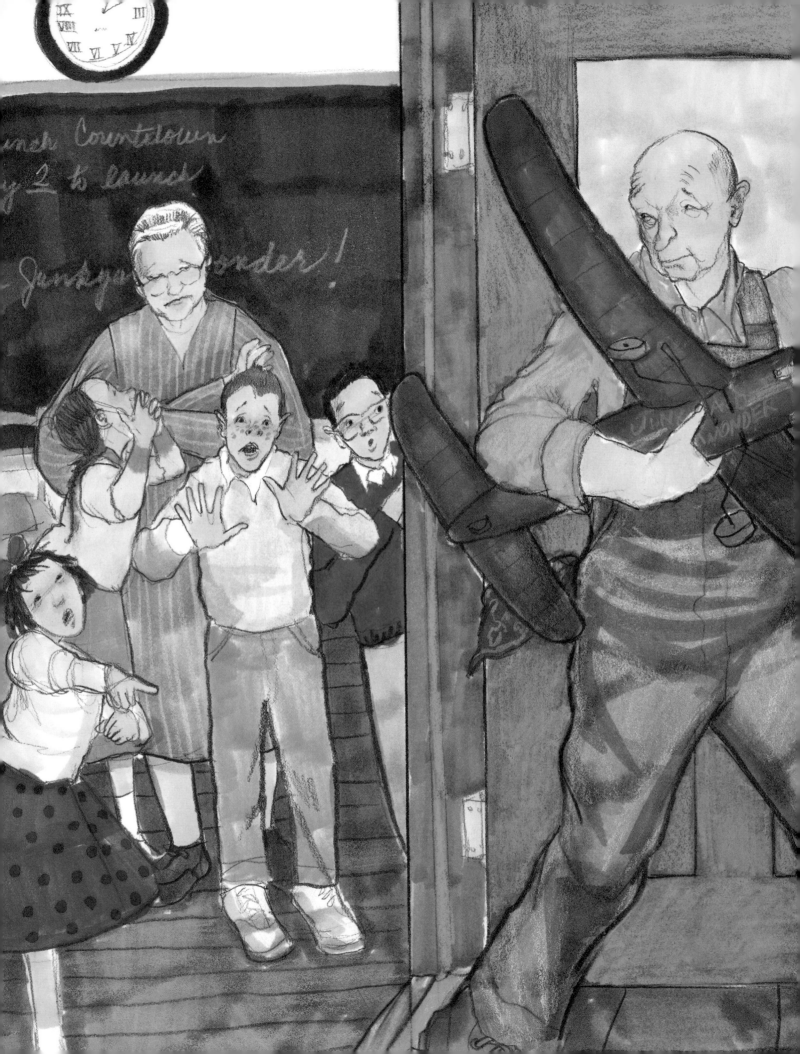

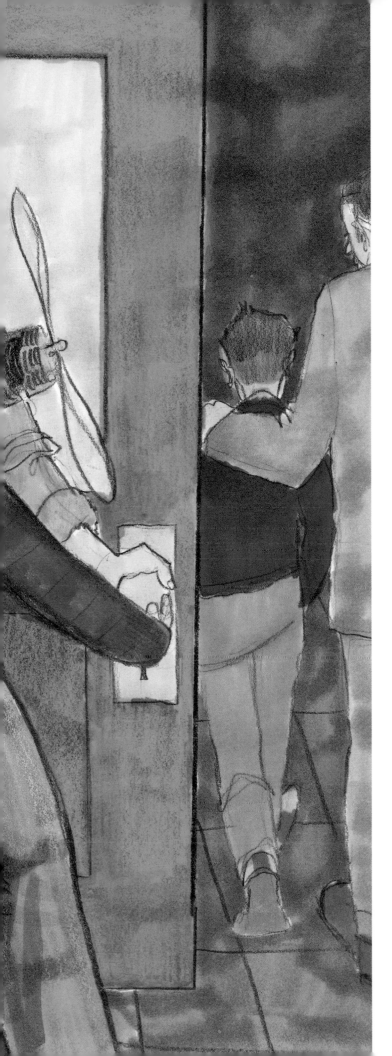

And sure enough, when we got back to our schoolroom, the principal was waiting for us, and Barton Poole was with him.

"I have been informed of your plans for the science fair, Mrs. Peterson. There will be no launching from the school roof, and no fuel-driven airplanes anywhere on the school grounds. It could be very dangerous. Mr. Weeks will keep your plane in the janitorial closet until the end of the school year." The principal turned on his heel and left the room.

Mr. Weeks looked very sad as he carried the Wonder out of the room. "Sorry, kids," he said.

We were stunned. Ravanne started crying. "This was going to be for Jody," she whispered.

Mrs. Peterson said nothing for a time, then she began, "We are going to launch the Wonder tomorrow . . . just as we planned. And from the roof!" Mrs. Peterson told us to be at Mr. Weeks' closet tomorrow morning, the morning of the fair.

Our secret weapon turned out to be Mr. McDonald, Gibbie's dad. If Mr. McDonald stayed with us during the launch, the principal was okay with it. We couldn't believe the good news.

Mr. Weeks handed the Wonder to Gibbie's dad. "Let's take her up," he said to us.

On the roof, we could see kids pouring onto the field to look at science exhibits that were being set up. Ravanne pulled gorgeous silk streamers that she had hand painted out of a bag and let them stay rolled up at the edge of the roof.

Then, with Thom's help, Gibbie and his dad put the Wonder in place. They carefully connected the engine to a car battery, then primed the pump to deliver the fuel from the tin sitting next to it into the engine. Then they pumped the fuel into the plane.

We all stood back and watched. "Maybe it'll go all the way to Lansing!" I speculated.

"Maybe even to Detroit," Thom said.

"Maybe around the whole world," Ravanne whispered.

"No," Gibbie said with a grin. "This baby is goin' all the way to the moon. . . ."

When the whole school assembled on the field, Mrs. Peterson signaled Gibbie's dad to begin the countdown to start the engine.

Mr. McDonald knelt in front of it while Gibbie held the plane still, spinning the propeller over and over again.

But the engine didn't catch on. We held our breaths.

"Pump the intake again," Mr. McDonald said to Gibbie. He asked some of the boys to hold on to the Wonder. "And you have to let it go at just the right moment or it will bank left or right. Understand?"

He spun the propeller a few more times, and then, with a loud bang and a roar, the propeller started spinning. Blue smoke puffed out.

Someone in the field yelled and everybody looked up at the roof. That was when Ravanne unfurled her banners down the side of the building.

"Almost to speed," Gibbie's dad hollered. "Ten, nine, eight . . ." When he got to one, Mr. McDonald hollered, "Let her go!"

The Junkyard Wonder shot out of everybody's hands. It was airborne!

First it went out over the field, then, as suddenly as it started, it sputtered and seemed to stall. Then the engine roared to life again with a noise that was deafening. The Wonder's nose pointed straight up . . . up and up . . . straight toward the sun.

We all ran to the wall of the roof and watched breathlessly as it streaked through the cloud cover, then appeared above. Ever skyward, straight to the stratosphere . . .

We all watched until it became a speck in the sky. Then we couldn't see it anymore.

Even though the science department from the local university was there, along with the school board and the newspapers, for all of us, it was only Mrs. Peterson that mattered. And Jody. Tears glistened in Mrs. Peterson's eyes as she watched the Wonder climb into the heavens.

"Like I said," Gibbie whispered, "that baby is going straight to the moon."

Mrs. Peterson has always been with me . . . all these years. So have all those in my tribe.

Thom went on to become the artistic director of the American Ballet Theater Company in New York. Ravanne became a textile designer and was eventually invited to Paris to design for the fashion industry. As for Gibbie, well, he went on to become an aeronautical engineer for NASA! He helped design the lunar modules for the Apollo missions. And me? I became a creator of books for children. For all of us, Mrs. Peterson was the wind beneath our wings. She was the alpha of our tribe. She was our compass!

I saw Gibbie in Houston a few years ago. We spent the afternoon recalling our time together in the junkyard and how Mrs. Peterson helped us believe in ourselves. Then Gibbie's eyes misted over. He leaned in to me and grinned as he said, "Remember that photo that my dad took of all of us that day on the roof, after we launched the Wonder? Well, Patricia, I stowed that photo aboard the lunar module on Apollo 11. All of us 'Wonders' really did make it to the moon after all."